MEARCSTAPA

MEARCSTAPA

BORDER-WALKER

Brainerd Prince

RUPA

Published by
Rupa Publications India Pvt. Ltd 2025
7/16, Ansari Road, Daryaganj
New Delhi 110002

Sales centres:
Bengaluru Chennai Hyderabad
Jaipur Kathmandu Kolkata
Mumbai Prayagraj

This is a work of fiction. Names, characters, places and incidents are either the product of the author's imagination or are used fictitiously and any resemblance to any actual person, living or dead, events or locales is entirely coincidental.

P-ISBN: 978-93-6156-607-3
E-ISBN: 978-93-6156-385-0

First impression 2025

10 9 8 7 6 5 4 3 2 1

Printed in India

Celebrating

Seeli and Prince

Parents, Fellow-Pilgrims

And all of you

who walk the borders

'In the tribal realities of earlier times, these [Mearcstapas or border-walkers] were individuals who lived on the edges of their groups, going in and out of them, sometimes bringing back news to the tribe.'

'Strider [the Ranger in *The Lord of the Rings*] is a *mearcstapa*, and it is in large part his ability to move in and out of tribes and boundaries that makes him an indispensable guide and protector and that helps him become an effective leader, fulfilling his destiny as Aragorn, high king of Gondor and Arnor, uniting two kingdoms.'

'*Mearcstapa* is not a comfortable role. Life on the borders of a group—and in the space between groups—is prone to dangers literal and figurative, with people both at home and among the "other" likely to misunderstand or mistrust the motivations, piety, and loyalty of the border-stalker.'

—Makoto Fujimura, *Culture Care*

Contents

Foreword

I am honoured to write the foreword for this book of poetry by my colleague and friend Professor Brainerd Prince. I have known Brainerd for just about three years, and yet I feel like I have known him forever. He is a quintessential mearcstapa, displaying amazing curiosity, grasp and humility while straddling several intellectual spheres, sometimes as sharply contrasting as religion and artificial intelligence. His mere presence in university meetings—where we often meet—elevates the discussion and brings down the walls between disciplines, enabling a free convergence of ideas otherwise alien to each other. I have come to know him as a rare combination of an intellectual nomad and a deeply rooted scholar. This book reflects this duality beautifully.

His poems are not only beautiful and profound but also reflect his deep engagement with the world and its challenges. He writes with honesty, compassion and courage, and invites us to share his vision and voice. Some of the poems are personal and intimate, exploring his own experiences, emotions and relationships. Some are inspired by his travels and encounters with different cultures and people. Some are political and social, addressing the issues of our time, such as war, poverty, injustice and environmental crises. Some are philosophical and spiritual, seeking to understand the meaning and purpose of life. Some are playful and humorous, celebrating the joy and wonder of existence. The collection is wide enough for anyone to find a personal resonance. The power of poetry gets you in the zone quite effortlessly, resonating with the soul of mearcstapa present in all of us. In the midst of reading these poems, I found myself thinking about border-walker atoms that diffuse through crystal lattices in materials and change their properties drastically even when they are small in numbers (e.g., doped semiconductors). Sometimes these influences have wonderful effects and sometimes quite deleterious. It does depend on the intention of the mearcstapa!

Throughout the book, the border-walker, the poet, goes in and out of so many disparate experiences and emotions, and yet the quest for a time and space invariant core seems all-pervasive. On the one hand, in 'My Mother's Son', the quest for a peaceful existence of togetherness cannot be missed in the following lines:

All we have are our words
Words that conjure up our realities
Words that create meaning
The very worlds in which we live
And so we desperately hope
That the words coming out of our mouth
Would become a home
Where we will live together

On the other hand, even such a noble quest is rendered irrelevant in 'The Ferris Wheel' when the poet writes:

The world never changed
It was, it is and will ever be
New eyes, new perspectives
New skin filling the seats
All that ended was your ride

There are several examples where the quest for the invariant core is unmissable, even when the border-walker is busy with the mission of his cross-border transactions. How relevant and apt is that to the times we live in! Technology has squeezed the world in which the different tribes of all kinds—professional–non-professional, political–apolitical, religious–areligious, engineers–doctors, artisans–scientists, and thousands of such others, have been pushed together much closer, making the life of the mearcstapa very busy. The quest for that space, then, where time melts away and the ever-changing world comes to a standstill, is the quest of every mearcstapa, every one of us.

Brainerd's *Mearcstapa* is a gift to all of us who love poetry and appreciate its power and beauty. I hope you will enjoy reading this book as much as I did, and discover the richness and diversity of Brainerd's poetry.

—Rudra Pratap
Vice Chancellor
Plaksha University

Introduction

I would like to claim that all human beings possess a dash of mearcstapa, even if they have lived a monocultural life, perhaps in a close-knit community. What I mean is that all of us humans inhabit multiple traditions—intellectual and embodied. This is due to the simple fact that while each human self is a unique locus of thinking and being in the world and is different from every other human self, it yet experiences diversity and plurality. Thus, within its unified self, there is a flow of many rivers. To some degree, even siblings and family members who live together face the 'other' amongst themselves. Diversity is not far off; rather it is inscribed in human nature.

The word mearcstapa has come to us from 'Beowulf', one of the most important Old English epic poems composed in the seventh century in the genre of Germanic heroic legends, about events that took place in the fifth and sixth centuries. In the poem, the term mearcstapa is used for Grendel and is translated as 'border-walker' or 'border-stalker'. Makoto Fujimura has made this term famous in his book *Culture Care: Reconnecting with Beauty for Our*

Common Life. This term has the imagery of 'living on the edges of traditions', with the 'ability to fluently move in and out of various groups and communities', living in the borderlands, in the interstitial spaces between diverse traditions. It is not necessarily a comfortable space to dwell in, often misunderstood by all groups. A mearcstapa can be homeless, both literally and figuratively, and a nomad, constantly moving between traditions of thought and practice.

On the other hand, a mearcstapa enjoys a rich life, which they intentionally fill with diverse heritages. They are polylingual and can engage in multiple language games. They are interpreters and translators of traditions—one to another—and enable 'deep connections' between diverse communities. A mearcstapa is necessarily a peacemaker, conflict-resolver and integrator. In our fast-paced present world, where the space between diverse traditions is shrinking, and often overlapping, we need many more of us to be a mearcstapa, to possess the ability to work with diverse ideologies, religions and traditions, to help humans understand one another and live harmoniously together. We need interpreters, translators and communicators who can straddle multiple identities, language games, and a plurality of intellectual and lived traditions to become polyglossic so that they can be guides to those who inhabit the deep centres of tradition.

I began by claiming that all humans possess a bit of the mearcstapa within us. Let me unpack that now: All of us inhabit multiple traditions, even when we inhabit the centres of the dominant tradition that defines our identity. The more we engage with our own tradition, the more we continue to remain at its centre. The more we develop the ability to look out, see the beyond, transcend the borders of our tradition and experience 'other' traditions, the more we move from the centre to the periphery or border. Most of us, loyal to our inherited or chosen traditions, choose to remain at its centre, and yet, every time we are faced with the 'other', we are forced to travel, even if it is just a little bit to keep a conversation going. In that conversation with the other, the mearcstapa within us comes to the surface, even if it is for a very brief moment and to a very low degree.

My research on Sri Aurobindo's integral philosophy focused on engaging two different and disparate ways of life: religious and secular traditions. Interestingly, this confluence of disparity is taking centre stage in our age of technology. We can experience this particularly in the field of education where there is a move to bridge the gap across the sciences, between science and humanities, as well as across the humanities. 'Interdisciplinarity' is the latest buzzword. Let me take an example from the world of engineering education. There was a time when professions were demarcated according to strict boundaries between various disciplines. A civil engineer was very different from a mechanical engineer who was very different from an electronic engineer. Their paths rarely crossed. However, today, on the one hand with the sweeping influence of new-age technologies and on the other hand with the complex problems faced by us humans and our planet, it has become imperative to transcend and cross over the borders of diverse disciplines. For example, a civil engineer today has to know not only about construction but also about energy conservation, which requires knowledge of AI-driven technologies. This is true not only for various kinds of engineers but also for all other professions. The complexities of our present world demand us to inhabit multiple intellectual and professional spaces to make any significant contribution.

Then there are a few of us who have made the borderland our dwelling and home either through circumstances or our choices. Being born a Tamil;

growing up in Delhi; having significant friendships and relationships with people from different parts of the country, particularly in Northeast India; having lived and worked in the UK, Southeast Asia and various parts of India; religiously born in a Christian family but with many meaningful relationships with people of other faiths, particularly Hindus; having done graduate studies in both Christian theology and Hindu traditions; being a member of both the Oxford Centre for Mission Studies and the Oxford Centre for Hindu Studies; and finally having done a PhD in the Humanities, in the philosophy of religion, and teaching in an engineering university has earned me the life of a mearcstapa. This echoes the old Sanskrit adage *neti neti*, 'not this, not this'—a wonderful way to describe a mearcstapa's non-belonging. And yet, in this 'non-belonging' to anyone, there is the 'embrace of the many'. The openness, the fluidity, the curiosity and the confidence to engage with ideas, structures and peoples who are different and make something powerfully new together. I am reminded of Walter Hollenweger's poem 'Prayer of the Frog' whose opening lines are as follows:

Sometimes, I feel like a frog,
Happy in the waterpond—until I run out
of air and creep on land.

Happy in the fresh air, until my skin
hurts in the glaring sun and
I plunge back into the water.
O God,
Why did you make me an in-between creature,
neither fish nor fowl?
Why am I not a flamingo, or an eagle or
a mighty roaring lion?
Just a frog?
[...]
So, I am, what I am, an in-between being.

The poems you will read in this book echo these words and spring from that hybrid, interstitial, conflictual space between traditions, out of the turmoil of being pulled and pushed between traditions. Perhaps in them, you will find an insight or two for the mearcstapa within you.

The Samaritan's Prayer

Philosopher: I was deeply thinking of prayer...

Theologian: Hmmm... What would he know about prayer, I wonder! In my reflection, prayer is...

The Samaritan: Come on, guys! Stop thinking and reflecting! Just pray!

My glorious eternal Lord
I come to You this morning
As a son to his father
As a disciple to his master
As a child to his teacher
As a servant to his Lord

I see You
Through my eyes of Faith
Through the eyes of my Mind
Through the imagination You have bestowed
Through the texts and traditions that follow Your name

As I gaze upon You
Your eternal undying self
Your glorious stately self
Your compassionate loving self

I sit, kneel and fall before You
Knowing I am wretched
Knowing I am not worthy
Knowing I am undeserving

I lay down at Your feet my brokenness
My pride and arrogance
My intellect, my service
All my past, my present, my future

Oh, dear lord
Master of this universe
Friend of sinners
Righteous judge
Accept Thou, myself, this sacrifice

now, oh, dear lord
speak and enunciate
in your thunderous glorious voice
in your small still voice

What do You think of me?
What do You want me to do?
Where do you want me to change?
How do you want me to live?

Speak, dear lord
Your servant is listening

Cobwebs

Cobwebs, oh the cobwebs
Poorly visible yet gloriously powerful

Beneath ornamental chairs and tables
Behind carved doors and French windows
Below exquisite curtains and linen falls
Between expensive furniture and walls

Cobwebs, oh the cobwebs
Gathering entangled hair-falls

Rich adorning beauty
In moments tarnishes
Revelling elegant lovelies
Suddenly vanishes

Cobwebs, oh the cobwebs
Reveal the spiders in our closets

Our Fashionable Age

We live in an age of fashion
A fashionable age, indeed
Not just an age of designer wear
But also of houses and hair

Fashion is not
Just a statement
A trillion-dollar industry, it is.
A divinity, perhaps a demigod
Demanding respect and regard

Wallets clapping with adulation
Credit cards bestowing blind devotion
All at the altar of fashion
In a long unending procession

No, it is no longer only
The Devil Wears Prada
Mere mortals like me and you
Of all classes, and races too

If originals are beyond reach
Copies of all ranks must do
First, second and even third
Any copy will do

But a bag must mean Gucci
A tie, definitely Versace
A car, only Maserati
In the garage a Lamborghini

Valentino dresses
Louis Vuitton leather
Balenciaga shoes
Nothing else will do

Even education
Has now become a fashion
Ivy League and Russell Group
Nothing else will do

Nothing short of designer babies
The trademark of our age
And yet we can't design our hearts
Our actions and our thoughts

Towards our neighbour, unfashionable
Old-school behaviour, unforgivable
Old-town violence, crusader rage
In our unfortunate fashionable age

The fashion show must go on
But not only of lingerie wear
Perhaps a showcasing of working together
A cocktail of sweat, toil and hard labour

A ramp walk of love and not of shame
A show-stopper not only of fame
We truly live in a designer age
So why not design a designer sage

A Tirade Against Historicality

You had your chance
All you now have are aches
You refused the crown
And looked the other way
She was here
Your desire to fulfil
But now she's gone, like the wind
Gone forever, never to return

But that is not the problem, is it?
If not, then what causes the worry?
Is it that she was not everywhere?
Her humanity unwilling to allow her
Curtailing, restricting, holding her down
One home, one school, one path of youth
Never a second chance, never more than once
This wretched *historicality*
This tunnelling of human abundance

Is it this limitedness that causes the mourning?
Is it this particularity who is the thief?
Oh how I wish her a thousand schools

A million families to grow in
To be ever-present everywhere
No time to mark her being
No space to confine her presence
Free to be everywhere
Free to be forever

But that is not possible, is it?
It is rather quite the impossible
Therefore we mourn
The death of infinite possibilities
And the passing away of the past
What we mourn
Is this fleeting human condition
Fated to particularity
Married to history
Never free to be

To be is but not to be

Farewells and Goodbyes

The sting of death
Is not in death itself
But in life
In that, life goes on
Unhindered, unencumbered
With full zest and exuberance
Even before we are hardly gone

Treasured and immortalized
In fading collective memory
But like *The Phantom of the Opera*
Doubly dead, mute and dumb
As the world parties into the night

In every farewell
In every goodbye
A glimpse we get
Of death itself
As we celebrate
A travelling away
The beginning of distance
The Presence of Absence

Trapped in Time

We are so trapped, the trappings have become us
We wear them, speak them, chew them, digest them
Children of history, yet it is the now
That has its stranglehold on us
The trappings woven so many times over
Glued to the skin, and penetrating beneath
No difference between
The trappings and the trapped
Like the scaffolding
Folded into the building

If being trapped is the human condition
And every attempt to escape
Only tightens the grip
Then the best of human intentions
With its rhetoric of escape and freedom
Embodied and ritualized in vain repetitions
Present only mirages of liberation

Then how is one to live? How is one to step out?
What should the self do? How should it be free?
What about the self's journey inward
Penetrating and piercing
Meticulously moving beyond

Every layer of trapping
Reaching beneath to touch one's skin,
One's flesh, one's very bone
And even the marrow below

Flesh meets flesh—the touch,
The touched and the toucher merge
Don't let any fool's rhetoric confuse you,
Nor allow yourself to be foolhardy
It is only in that moment of self-touch
Can one see the beyond
The beyond of the self and the trappings
And in that sight one flies
Leaving the trappings behind

A Holiday from Myself

Even before I wake up
I am already someone, somebody
Some I want to be, most I don't
I am a father, a brother, a son
A wife, sister, mother
Roles I was born with
Promotions I didn't demand
Doctor, architect, lawyer
Banker, florist, cab driver

A character in a drama
A part I didn't consent to play
A script I didn't write
Keeps me firmly entwined

Time keeps turning the pages
And the story ceaselessly continues
Roles I am forced to play
Even when I resist and refuse
All I do is crawl into another story

The plot again is already set
Little change can I bring
Not just the plot of the dramas I play

But the master plot, the mother of all plots
The plot of the story itself

It is tiring to play these roles
Enact all these parts
Scripts to voice
Rituals to play
Practices to perform
Tiring, exhausting, all-consuming

I need out, I need a holiday
I need a place to recuperate
But if I am the parts I play
And I am the roles I perform
Then how do I escape and run

I need a holiday from myself
From all parts and roles
Even from stories that give significance
And narratives that provide meaning

But how can that be?
How can one flee from oneself?
Even death does not provide a way of escape
As long as the story continues and the drama plays
I live on and continue to perform
Even after death in the memory of time

If even death cannot set me free
How else can I fly?
Move past the constraints
Placed by the characters
Roles I am forced to play
Into the wilderness, I must go
Into the wilderness, I must disappear
The blackhole of narratives
The death of the story
The oblivion of meaning

I yearn for the wilderness
To strengthen, to refresh
To help me understand
To be beyond me
To be truly me

Stop Reading Any Further

Stop
Stop reading, I say
You don't want to know
You really don't

And yet you read

But, why?
Why do you read on?
Why can't you just stop?
STOP! Stop reading, I beg!

I am sure you are NOT reading this

Alas, I am wrong
You are still reading!

What can I do to make you stop?
Make you give up, abandon
Move on as if you have not read
I say don't but still you do

But you can't help yourself, can you?
Can't stop, even if you want to
Because it's not really you

That needs to be stopped
It's actually not even about you, is it?

It's the words seeking their whole
Semantic unity, they say
Half in your consciousness
The others in the lines below
Condemned to meaning
A tyranny, not a travesty
'Memes!' exclaims Dawkins, with glee
But it's the mother of memes
The one who bore them
The eternal goddess!
Do you not fathom?

词 λόγος शब्द Word
Call it what you may
She lives on forever
In and through you
And of course
Before and beyond you

Humans come, humans go
Yet she lives on
Ancient of days
Creating, destroying, recreating
Forming, re-forming, multi-forming

Tower of Babel, mustn't forget
Nor the Pentecost

Regaining regal power
In her being
The universe came to be
She lifted her voice
And the walls came tumbling
She has seen the beginning
And in her is the end
You and I
Her playmates in time
Must stop now
Can't let her always
Go on winning, can we?

My Mother's Son

I have never seen her
Although her eyes I have, they say
Her voice too I have never heard
But I was told she sang like a bird
I was told she was very beautiful
Her skin soft as snow
Her form that graced a thousand stars
Defined beauty for us, you know

She had to leave, however
They came and took her away
In the middle of the night
They packed her out
Left my father in a pool of tears
And while she grabbed my brother
I was left behind

I haven't seen them since twenty-five years
My father long passed by
Neither did he ever again
See his other son and wife
We got her regular letters for sure
And growing pictures of my brother

But her face, we never got to see
Not in a postcard, or a glimpse ever

I grew up in Damascus
The oldest city that ever was
As Syrian as one could get
Yet I was both Muslim and Christian
Speaking Arabic, French and English
Never crossed the Mediterranean Sea
Nor into the Iraqi desert I strayed
Lebanon kept me hemmed in
While Israel watched my borders

A true Arab, I told myself
I was born to live and lead
To help my people live in the desert
And not to cross over
In the land of my ancestors
We loved our music and our women
We are an old people, you know
A lot to learn, in order to live
Even if we are stubborn

And then my brother did come to visit
But alone he did not come
He came with schools and cars
And eyelids studded

With a new education
A lack of knowledge
He said, was our blindness
I showed him our ancient cuneiform
And treasures rivalling the best of Egypt
The land that groomed Cicero's teacher
And the writings out of Apamea

He persisted that we need to be civilized
With genuine concern and a dismissive hand
With our protests came out his guns
The warning, clear and loud
You better heed
For your own good, or else

Then one day he came to visit me
To my village, and to my home
I made a feast to welcome him
And invited the village in
With their *dabkeh* they greeted him
And their sword dances sought to woo
The food was spread with splendour
The houses adorned with lights
It was magical yet not mystical
As real as any summer evening can be
My neighbours showered their love
Total strangers hugged and kissed him

They made him feel at home
He forgot he was the other
He began to move and shake his leg
And forgot he was near Aleppo

I took a step backwards
Away from the dancing crowd
To watch my mother's son dance
His movements not dissimilar to mine
Although it's been twenty and five long years
I was seeing him for the first time

He was not so other
In spite of all the differences
Our views of our worlds in which we live
And the stories we tell each other
May seem as far as the east is from the west
But in our bodies, and in our movements
In our quests for life, in our very existence
A blood-knit kindred spirit we shared

I took his hand, drew him from the dance
We walked into the setting sun
Without a word on our lips
Twin brothers were we
Our beloved mother's womb we had shared
Under our father's watchful eye
And entangled, we entered this world

The time to speak has at last come
To open our mouths in utterance
The power lay in the language we use
As we seek to understand the other
To kill or to live and to let live
The pen is mightier than the sword, it's said
And words more mighty than the pen
All we have are our words
Words that conjure up our realities
Words that create meaning
The very worlds in which we live
And so we desperately hope
That the words coming out of our mouth
Would become a home
Where we will live together
For better or worse
For richer or poorer
In sickness and in health
To love and to cherish
Brothers, sons of the same mother

The Angry Young Man Must Die

Oh, how I will miss him!
But he must go
Only to remain in memory
But dead to the world
Dead to me
And yet I will miss him

He sure was
The ideal of my life
Taking the world head on
Fearless and restless
Anger and rage
Spilling forth generously
Yet a keen eye
Always looking out
For the underdog
For the weak, the broken-hearted
Defending the helpless
Fighting their battles
Tired, and yet fuelled by anger
The anger flourished

He took on the strong
Pushed back their lines
Gained respect
But even more hatred
From the strong
They hit back hard
And drove him out
And the murderous anger matured
Its venom spewed forth
Harming everything
Relentlessly, passionately

Caught between the fires
The powerful mocked
The helpless agitated
Fighting to the left
Fighting to the right
Anger, oh anger, everywhere

That is why he must go
Small battles won
But the war long lost
He must die
The weak and the strong
Have already killed him
He must decidedly die

The sun must set

Maybe in death
He finds redemption
Anger is not passion
It destroys rather than builds
Passion possesses care
Anger is not vision
It blinds the far-sighted
Vision is compassion
Anger is not motivation
It demoralizes the most motivated
Motivation is but love

Anger births hatred
It is crude, harsh, destructive
There is no place for anger
Even for righteous anger
No right to anger, nowhere
All anger destroys

That is why he must die
It is in his death that
The helpless will see wisdom
The powerful learn compassion
But for that he must die
And I will miss him

But the angry young man
Must die

Strange Bedfellows or Strangers in Bed

Hey, would you care to listen?
Whether we have known each other
For a day or a myriad of years
Whether we are strangers in love
Or eternal bedfellows
Whether every sight of the other
Tingles excitement
Or mundane ordinariness rules the day
Will you not reach out to squeeze my hand?

Each time I share excitedly
The treasures I have scavenged
Even if words obscure and falter
Will you not lend me your ear?
Will your eyes not glisten with my stories?
Will you not reach out to wipe my tears?
And hold me tight each time I shudder?
Or smile knowingly as my face bewilders?

It's my pain that I share
Shattered visages of my ancestors
I am but my past

And it is my past that has been defied
Shrouded with the blackness of a full moon sky
Soiled in the trenches of London
Trampled by Her Majesty's horses
In tatters, I find my Self
Broken, squashed, darkened
My Self, the memory of my history
Can I dare to dream?
Of rewriting histories?
Of mending memories?
Of remembering my Self?

But how should it begin?
Where do I start?
If it's my present that frames my past
Then won't it begin with you and me?
I hold on as you brace me up
We tell stories out of suitcases
And pack new memories neatly
Back in those old cases
Talk into the night about distant lands
About ancient cities, roaring warlords
The rich and the poor
The prince and the maiden
Of children crawling up to their fathers

Of babes clinging to their mothers
Suckling calves in the yonder farms
Stories of love, anger and pain
We go up, up and around
In this Ferris wheel—
The tragedy of life

As we talk and laugh
Wipe the silent tear
Memories refreshed
The Self strengthened
The lamb will lie with the lion
As the suitcases move away
Widening distance, they carry
You and me, together, forever

The Dancing Mares

Out they came in the hundreds
Galloping, snorting, heads held high
Arabian, Ardennais and *Akhal-Teke*
Let loose from Odin's own land
Messala's and Ben Hur's royal steeds
Thundering down Rome's Circo Massimo

Chariots, coaches and carts in tow
Bridles and bits
Adorning their magnificent faces

Reaching Troy's splendid gates
Dusted their hooves
Unhitched all trappings
Entered the Assembly
In grand array

The most beautiful of meetings
Horses, horses everywhere
All colours, shapes, all sizes
Without bridle, without bits
Free from carriages, free from chariots

King Stallion took his place
Brought the meeting to order with his hooves
The most amazing of horse-music floated
Filling the expanse of the fresh Sunday morn

Wondrous of sights, graceful forms
The mares took to beat
Raising their front hooves
Balancing on their hind
One two three, one two three
The mares began to sway
The tempo picked...the beat got louder
Mares and horses
Faster and faster
Glorious, astounding
Oh, the dancing reverential mares
Sun down, lengthening shadows
The moon begins to rise
The gong sounds
The assembly dispersed
Through Troy's tall gates
Outside its daunting walls

Bridles and bits back in place
Chariots, coaches and carts in tow

Back they galloped into Rome
Sunday is over, Monday is back
To drive and be driven
To Caesar's land

Beaches of Bournemouth

As you lift your gaze and look at her
There she stands—majestic, royal
Brimming with confidence
With resilience and life
In her calmness
In the clarity of her deep blue self
You see creation in its magnificence
The immovable mover
The Being at its best

You take a step closer
Watch her in proximate spaces
Beneath the calmness
A million moves
A constant weaving of waves
From horizon to horizon
Her beauty stretches
Her joyous spirit
Bursting forth in a thousand shades
Exploding with wondrous energies
Dancing light steps on still shores
She is restless, moving constantly
Being is but Becoming
Change and movement

Through the process of time

The night draws in deep
The moon is out and loud
She takes hold of the winds
And makes them her own
Wave and wind in rhythm
The most marvellous of music floats
Creation stands enchanted
Picks the beat of her spirit
Swirling round and round
Oh, what an astounding sight
All of creation in tune
Singing and dancing
Laughter and joy everywhere
She lifts her head and smiles
The Shamrock Bar comes to life

The morning has broken
The sun seeps through the clouds
And sunlight skips upon her waves
The blue turns golden
A new day, a new beginning
Calmness reigns, yet unleashed
Strength in silence
Storm in stillness
Being and Becoming
The twin existence of life

Be the Wind-Paint: Reflections on Year-ends

Flowing from one box to another
Life pigeonholed into tight boxes
Neatly labelled day, month and year
Defining mornings and noontimes
And telling you when to go to bed

As I flow out from one year-box into another
You tell me, it's an occasion for celebration
Look back at the number of boxes you have filled,
you say
With memories both trivial and pearls
Look how you have repeatedly traversed harm's way
And painted life, red, purple and blue

And yet all I feel is old

A new box has many adventures, you say
New space, new time
Life in your hands
And the sky, your limit, you exclaim

But you forget, it's into another box I flow
It's not just me filling out the box

It's the box filling me out as well
The box squeezes me in, its walls cramping
Rubs the colour off me onto herself
She defines what I do and even how I look
When tired of me, she pushes me out
And December comes a-ringing

You should go celebrate
Sure, do ring those nice bells
And, don't forget your prayers
Be happy that you have filled this box
Ready to climb into another
Beginnings and ends are sure reasons for celebration
So, go ahead and put on that dress

But I am going to linger a bit longer
Raise a glass to you
And wonder how I can get rid
Of this damn box staring at you
Burn its walls down
Blaze them all out
Push it forward
Create a domino effect
Destroy all boxes with one big push
Then none to fill
Into none I'll flow

And then think about how I can be the wind
That can just be
Always flowing
And yet needless to flow
And when I do flow, no one needs to know
No box to constrain, no walls to cramp
The sky, the canvas and me the wind-paint

Blood on My Hands

I have killed them
Murder it was, definitely
Watching them die helplessly
Tried my best to save them
Hearing death's deadly tune
I paced the floor up and down
Changed waters by the dozen
Care and medicines
None withholding
But nothing I did
Could save them

Three mates were they
An incredible trio I must say
When morning broke
There remained but two
There was panic in their world
As they circled the slain
Coping with their pain
Sadness unfeigned
Watching them experience
The loss of breath
I experienced death

As I helped with the funeral
Nagging thoughts unfolded
Cold-hearted murderer
Was I not responsible?
Was I not the killer?
Was it not my water they drank?
Swum in my tank
My food they ate
My air sealed their fate
Was I not responsible?
Was I not the killer?

I watched them looking at me
Their gait greatly reduced
Lethargic, unusually quiet
No appetite, unseduced by food
Should've taken that as a sign
As winter fast approached
With playfulness all but gone
I thought 'twas the cold
What else could it be but the chill?
That shrivels the living to the bone
But those tiny powerful eyes
They kept staring
Recollecting good times
Memories reminiscing
Maybe pleading

To be set free
Maybe foreseeing
Changes in their destiny

The noonday sun
Burned dim
The clouds cast their spell
She had suddenly gone still
I rose with panic under my belt
Knocked on the glass panes
Shook with might to inject life
Circling around their home
Sensing a loss in the fight
What should I do?
How should I be?
The breath all but gone
Final moments prolonging pain
Helpless about helplessness
Every breath now tedious
Nothing I could do would help
I turned my face
And she was gone
Ha, ha, mocked Macbeth
You too now have blood on your hands

Only the big man remained
Golden glistening skin
Majestic in stride

He is powerful
A fighter who will surely survive
Overcome cruel fate
The sun disappeared
A shroud of darkness
Blanketed space
Humans light a million suns
Pushing darkness backwards
The big one had suddenly gone cold
But I could do nothing onwards

With a heavy heart
I watched till I could watch no more
Eyes closing, I went to sleep
I woke up as the sun rose strong
Rested through the night
Drove away darkness at dawn
I turned to see
Behold, he too was gone

I paused as I gazed through
The windowpanes
One last time
Was I responsible?
Was I their killer?
Three beautiful creatures
Gone now, all dead

The Elusive You

I wake up every morning, looking for you
Searching for your face, in the faces I view
At the bus stop, down the garden path
City centre or some far corner

Every party I go to, every club to dine
In all the forms and colours, all the people I find
Looking for you, searching for you
Looking over my shoulder, all the time

There, I find you, then I don't
You seem to be there, but I miss seeing you
All around me I see your face
Yet never ever your sweet embrace

Rising with emptiness, racing eyes, longing soul
Dragging through dangerous dark alleyways
And along sweet country roads
Straining, searching, yet never ever finding

Waking Up

You see yourself lying
Asleep on the bed
The world consists of
The room in your house
And the house in the neighbourhood
Your city and country, come to view
A final zoom
And hey, the continent, and the planet
Boom, this the world is

You gently move
As dawn breaks free
With light playing tricks on your face
The curtains slowly draw
Eyes open and yet not wide
Your world comes to life
You see yourself
And the world
Sad, apathetic or ecstatic
The passions surge
Glimpses merge
Of people, things and ideas
Shapes animated, lighted up

Your world begins to move
Actions, movements, things to do
Take colour as the sun streams through
A movie you see
With you seeing it, in it
Personality for people
Desires for things
Moods for places
All fill the screen
Your world is alive
Awake and throbbing
Yet with eyes still closed
You remain in your bed
Time to wake up
To open those eyes wide
To fit the furniture of the universe
Into your world
That is already alive

The Ferris Wheel

Round and round went the Ferris wheel
Birth, life, death in motion
What comes around goes around
Only to come back again
The wheel climbs higher
Horizons growing, eyes conquering
Perspectives change, and the thrill of control
Breath held tight, heart beats wild
You are the dancing queen
With the big wide world
In the palm of your hand
But in a second
Down she comes, the wind in your skirts
Gravity beckons, vision contracts
The world disappears
Just the Thames in your eyes
Perspectives change, losing control
Slower and still slower
Until the eye shuts
The fairies bid farewell
You are on the ground
Another takes your seat
And the wheel gathers speed

Everything remains as is
The world never changed
It was, it is and will ever be
New eyes, new perspectives
New skin filling the seats
All that ended was your ride

A World Without Me

I see a world without me
Just as busy and green
The sun rising and setting
Its usual course following
Cities bustling, bursting at the seams
Lethargic countryside lazing

The newspapers, bold their headlines
Internet editions, change by the hour
No mention of me
No mention of my existence
Life goes on
As it always has been
Maybe there is a mention
Tucked in between the pages
A little obituary
A little gathering by a graveside
With a few black clothes hired
The cars drive away
I am left alone
All gone, and so am I

Did I exist?
Or was it all a dream?
A few ol' pictures, a drawer full of papers
A character in a few memories
Blurry, growing fuzzy, as the plot fades
With me dead, I am but an object
A bit of ash for keepsake
A bounded entity now
Left behind in memory
With me gone
The objects begin to play

Who said objects don't grow?
Expand and increase
In innumerable ways
It is now that I am immortalized
Never to die
Never to leave
Always to be
Forever to grow old
With the ageing world
Only when I am
Truly no more

Desperate Revolutions

Revolutions come
In all shapes and sizes
With added colours
For the camera
Fun frills for the ride
Scientific
Industrial
Political
Freedom from religion
Brought enlightenment
Freedom from slavery
Yes, look, we are genuinely free
Freedom from sexuality
Liberated roles and orientations
But nothing new under the sun
Revolutions have always defined
The human race
They exist
From ancient days
But hark, listen
There is something new
A rumble in the air
A thunder

That never before clapped
A view of the world
That you alone have
With the click of a mouse
Behold, view the whole world
Knowledge of its history
Power to divinize its posterity
And yet
The view circumscribes
The limits of humanity
Visions beyond the glasshouse
Can be seen but never reached
Nowhere to go
Nothing more to live for
Nothing satisfies
Any longer
Cheap thrills they feed us
Money, jobs and holidays
Invent dreams
Boring routines
Fed up with progress
Have lived it
Vicariously
Success has lost its charm
Materiality its glitter
Work its purpose

Holidays their thrill
If this is to be human
Then tired of being one
Hence this revolt
From New York to London
Stepping blithely
From Bahrain to Egypt
Not for freedom
Not against ideology
Against humans, it is
The revolt
Against Humanity

Plea for a Broken World

When the very earth you stand on and build your dreams
Shivers and crumbles
It is good

When the very air you breathe turns toxic
And causes you to gasp
It is good

When the very relationship that gives you a home
Rends asunder
It is good

When the very narrative in which you are the lead character
Fragments into oblivion
It is good

The worlds we build need to collapse
How else will the foundations be re-formed
The foundations need to smither
How else will their material be examined

Unless life crumbles
Its conditions won't surface
Its imaginaries remain hidden
The mechanisms that automate our lives
The engines that wheel us through
The structures that dominate
Can only be examined and re-formed
In a broken world

Life at Cross Tracks

Ideas and dreams
Steering wheel of life
Life fashioned, subjugated
Moulded in shape
Held strong, bound within
Stories lived are but stories told
Mimetic life yet thriving on vision

Life springs forth
Not in isolation, not alone
Community of selves
Conversation, revelation, communion
New ideas, new dreams
Different stories, changing visions
Stories told are but stories lived
Life births ideas
Cradles in its bosom
Shapes and moulds
Fixes into its likeness

How great the love
Life and idea

Each shaping the other
Embrace long and intimate
Each other's children

Idea birthing life
Life birthing idea
The new idea gains form
And the mould breaks
At that moment
Mimesis explodes

New tracks being laid
New stories written and told
Old and new cross over
Life waits patiently
How to live, what direction to take
Standing still at cross tracks

The Potter's Wheel

I shared my life with her and she left me
I dreamt our life together and now she is gone
As I turned and watched and looked beyond
The glorious sun setting for once broke my heart
Every waking hour
A gift wrapped me, her I gave
Every breath was hers to keep
But she left me, disappeared
Crying out as she left, never to return
As I watched her storm through the window
A part of me left with her
As I braced my life and pulled in my breath
I knew she couldn't go far
It's the horizon we share
As the sky reaches from the east to the west
And touches us wherever we be
It is that sky, the same universe
The one whole of which we are but parts
That holds us, embraces us
In our absence, there is presence
In our loneliness, togetherness
Forms are created, forms perish
Like clay in a potter's hands

A thousand forms, a million designs
Clay is one and yet is all
Forming and deforming
Round and round the potter's wheel
How else do we live with separation?
How else do we account for brokenness?
It's in the breaking
That we are formed
Once more, yet again
It's the distance
That draws and maintains
The unity of the soul
As I gaze out of the window one last time
Holding back my pain, my haunted sorrows
Flashing images of good times, great times
If I had the legs to move and hands to grasp
Would I not run after, would I not embrace?
But there I lie lifeless
It is I who had left, I who had stormed out
The form had broken, time run out
I can see myself looking through the window
Everybody there, the universe together
She will be fine, I tell myself
She has a life full to live
A beautiful vessel is she
The potter's favourite shape

Gold to hold, gems to keep
Destiny beckons her and live must she
To make music, to make love
To write out a script
For the dear potter to spin
Much to do much to live for
Life has begun and it sure must go on
Even as I left, fading in the far distance
I knew for sure, I was certain
Unformed takes form again
In brokenness, there is new creation
The universe holds us together

Two Bags and a Rucksack

On a journey am I
From dawn to dusk
And yet again to dawn
Walking, trudging, moving all the time
Climbing over mountains, wading across rivers
Skipping through meadows, rolling down grassy hills
Through the forests, or in the city bright
I am always on this voyage
This life expedition
With two bags and a rucksack
My constant companions

The bag on the right contains my life
Some call it soul while others spirit
Pneuma, Geist, Chi or *Brahman*
It is you, me and the entire universe
From my bag, working in me
Energizing, expressing, living

The bag on the left contains my memories
Stories of all my journeys
Beautiful people I have met
Places I have been, the love I have shared

The kindness I have received
These are the many tales of the journey
The story of the spirit
Mine, yours, the chronicle of the universe

I drag these bags with their precious treasures
I keep plodding from one morning to another

The rucksack on my back
Contains my earthly belongings
The things I call mine
House deeds, jewellery, traveller's cheques
Money in many currencies, land and gold
All my possessions, in the rucksack, on my back

Sometimes the bags get heavy
And my back gets bent
The memories turn horrid
The spirit cold and low
And the journey becomes a drag

But then the spirit rises again
Swells up with life and light
With the rising sun
Am game to give up all my possessions
My gold and my diamonds
The rucksack I will gladly forsake

More beautiful memories I'll make
The bags become one
Memories are the history of the spirit
When all is gone
I am but my memory

Tears

Have you cried lately
And allowed the tears
To stream by
It feels like there is
A pressure
In the chest
That only tears can let fly
It is not a pain of grief
Nor one of loss
It is the facing of the
Unexpected
That brought forth
Tears, unexpected
A pleasant surprise
A need fulfilled
A wish granted
A glimmer of hope
Against all odds
From unexpected quarters
Unexpected
Memory does its bit
Digs out
Resonant experiences

The event takes
A grand scale
Behold
The hand of God
At work
Mysterium magnum
Everywhere
Meaning-making begins
Cultural narratives kick in
To God be the glory
Hare Rama Hare Krishna
Subhanallah
Maybe even
Gan Xie Zhu
Sláva Bógu
Kyrie Eleison
The tears keep streaming
Gently down the cheeks

Go Figure Destiny

You have to do it
No one can stop you
No school, no education
No fancy guitar classes
It's you facing your demons
Hell-raisin' experiences
You breaking that wooden door
Getting out, exploring more
Learning to stand
On your two small feet
While still drinking
Your mother's sweet
Facing your father
Who is no longer there
And your mother
Who fancies cars
More than your care
Bidding goodbye
To the good boys at school
I'd rather be gay
Than pretend playin' fool
You work your shit
No one told you it would work

Shaping your spirit
Embodying perils
You go find a home
I go figure destiny

Time

Time is not
A number on the watch
Nor the ticking of a clock
Neither a position
Of the sun
Nor the movement of the stars
It's not a string of seconds
Nor an accumulation of moments
It is immeasurable
Non-quantifiable
Uncontrollable
132 minutes
Can live out two centuries
Days could be but moments
Years like weeks
A whole lifetime
But a few seconds
Or
You can count aloud
Every damn second
And watch the hands tick
Till the eyes with tears swell
Yell, cry and scream

Stomp as loud as you will
But the hour will never rush
Even nightfall will remain
As bright as day

The Dark Side of Good

Ominous fragrance-soaked air
Measured movements in black
Heaving chests, long sighs
Silent gasps and cries
Loud without sound
Dance without the dancer
Strings vibrate long notes
Air heavy with anticipation
White lilies adorning
Every parlour chair taken
No room even to stand
The water breaks
Her heaves cease
Behold the murderer is born
Celebration turns into mourning
Cries of joy mixed with grief
No doubt she doesn't know her crime
Like so many lives including mine
Parasitic on others for ours to live
Life and death connected extraordinaire
Each fuelling the other
Why scapegoat a few
For this monstrous arrangement

Why imprison or shoot at sight?
Even sincere benevolence
Experiences metamorphosis
Eager for the good it seeks for the other
It gets rid of the filth
Re-forming the scum of the earth
Scrubbing clean the baby
Skin peels, blood flows
Scrubs harder
The baby screams in agony
But cleanliness is next to godliness
And the scrubbing continues
Is it self-affirmation?
One's purity displayed
Or is it the cruel dialectic
Between self-worth and the worth of selves
My worth determined
By the worth I force on the other
Or even self-redemption?
I need to stand for good
The overcoming self
Recompensing my evil
But the march for good
This glorious crusade
Soon rots into evil
Oh the unrestrained violence of good

Numinous hatred and sacred brutality
Or just the plain evil of the self
Sorry tales we tell ourselves
Pass them on to our children
Create characters in supporting roles
The villain, always the other
Poor, ugly bastards
Needs stamping out as roaches
Unleashing uncontrolled
The power of my good
My licence to kill
Good and evil
Illegitimate categories
Yet needed for sanity
In this insane universe

Passion Lasts Forever

Fell in love
But soon
Failed in love
She was engaged
Secretly to another
Sent to be a dealer
Family wanted him
Wheeling and dealing
To Paris was he sent
In 1875
Art or commodity
Perverse vulgarity
Resentment led to
Termination
Fled Paris
For England
Turned to religion
And at last
Found his passion
This is what I want to do
True vocation mine to stay
But failed again
Entrance exams

Couldn't clear
Okay then, a smaller post, but
Failed again
No diploma, not even a certificate
No chance
For even a tiny portion
Of the dream
Imagine
Couldn't be a doctor
Not even a nurse
Not even an attendant
There is no room
In the hospital
But passion dies hard
Especially when
Kicked down by defeats
The force of the failures
Fuels its flames
The dream it meant to destroy
Resurrects with strength
Onwards to *Petit-Wasmes*
Borinage, Belgium
Into the coal mines
Living like a miner
Slept on straw-spread floors
Behind the baker's door

Foxes have holes
Birds have nests
But all he had was
Sobs and tears
But failure strikes again
Got kicked out
Of the coal mine
For undermining
The dignity of
The dream
Custodians of the dream
Guardians of the Church
Or art dealers from Rome
Family found him crazy
Sent him to an asylum
At *Geel*
Failed in love
Failed in dealing
Failed in religion
But the passion
Kept burning
Changed form
But kept burning
Turned to art
In the service of God
Some capture in words

But I will do pictures
Maybe the good times
Are at last in, rolling
Love seems to come knocking
No sooner, the notion
Old friend failure screams
Niet, Nooit, Nimmer
Failures come in all kinds
But the greatest of these is love
The preacher turns to a prostitute
To Sien's bosom for love
Love she did
Gonorrhoea he caught
Failure comes back visiting
Sardonic smiles
Passion inflamed
Turns menacing
He paints her with his brush
The art turns violent
To God be the glory
Gordina de Groot
Is pregnant
Time is running fast
How long would passion last?
The pictures and the prostitutes
Came fast, rapidly working his brush

Chased from the hospital
Not to be a doctor
Neither nurse nor attendant
He came back in
As a patient
For the asylum, he sought
Fou roux was he called
The red-headed madman
Friends and family desert
And failure promptly returns
For a last visit
Shot through his chest
At thirty-seven
Revolver he held
With his own hand
Passion ebbing
Twenty-nine long hours
Cigarette reaching its butt
Flicker ready to snuff
Closed his eyes
And out came the
Famous last words
'The sadness
Will last
Forever'
A madman, menacing

Died a pauper
With no lover
To hold his hand
But sadness is passion re-formed
Passion lasts forever
Who would have thought
The unloved was a father
Expressionism
His true begotten child
Today worth in billions
He dwells amongst the rich
Famous he makes the ordinary
The ordinary has become famous
Millions call on his name
His pictures enframe their souls
The final battle commences
Failure charges passion
Passion flares its nostrils
A flick of the brush
A throw of the wrist
A death blow it receives
And Failure falls to its knees
Failure fails to conquer
Receives a sardonic stab to the chest
Passion snuffs failure
Passion never dies
Passion lasts forever

Portmanteau

Do I not fit into
Your nice little box?
Neither the circular
Nor the square

You try very hard
Stuffing me in
Neatly packing
All pieces within

And yet they explode
Bursting open the seams
Like an overpacked
Portmanteau

Like a strutting peacock
Impossible to contain
Impossible to tame
Impossible to name

Gratitude

Being happy with our life today
Living without regrets of the past
Looking forward to a bright tomorrow

If these be the goals of life, then it all begins
With an attitude of thankfulness and gratitude

I am grateful for the gifts I have received
I am grateful for the challenges I have endured
I am grateful for the people present in my life
I am grateful for those who have come and gone by
I am grateful for the doors opened by the opportunities lost
I am grateful for the accidents and illnesses
I am grateful for the un-shot arrows
I am grateful that I am breathing
I am grateful for the little joys that bring smiles and laughter
I am grateful that the sparrows are truly well

Does Life Matter?

It is the mountains we envy
The sun whose life we covet
The grandiose galaxies spanning the universe
It is they of whom we are truly jealous

Each of them has watched humanity
Like a mother over a child
With a smile and a laugh, they observe
How humans come, play, and go by

Alexander the Great, Akbar the Great and Alfred the Great
Jerusalem's King David and Babylon's King Nebuchadnezzar
Built empires that flourished, plateaued and perished
All under these ever-eternal, watchful eyes

As for man, his days are truly like grass
As a flower of the field, so he flourishes, sprouts anew
When the wind has passed over, he is no more
He fades and withers; no one remembers him any more

Therefore, with each death we imagine our own ending
Dust to dust, we are condemned to oblivion
We weep for the dead, perhaps more for ourselves
The tragedy of human life; it is always too soon gone

And yet the body remains, a powerful symbol of a life once lived
Finally immortalized, finds her eternal home
As the earth opens herself up to welcome and receive
With the sun, moon and the stars in perpetual attendance

Living Again

I have cried my tears
Oh, cried a river dry
I have walked
The *Via Dolorosa*
And said my goodbyes

I have spent all my grief
Emptied all my pains
Pauper, lying prostrate
With no tears left to shed
Tired and exhausted
A sea of sorrows swam I

Like a phoenix rising from its ashes
A newborn birthing from the womb
Clothed in regalia, crowned with flowers
I see you stand
With the glory of the rising sun
And the radiance of the red moon

Then I crumble, falling to my knees
Empty pockets, penniless
With nothing left to give
Yet the sun beckons me with its rays
And the moon, splendidly charming
Summons me with its light display

The Sayings of Agur, the Son of Jakeh

These sayings are not just inspired utterances but also possess provocatively insightful humour. For example, take these sayings:

'The leech has two daughters.
"Give! Give!" they cry.'

or

'There are three things that are never satisfied,
four that never say, "Enough!":
the grave, the barren womb,
land, which is never satisfied with water,
and fire, which never says, "Enough!"'

or

'For as churning cream produces butter,
and as twisting the nose produces blood,
so stirring up anger produces strife.'

Now one of my own, constructed in the style of Agur, the son of Jakeh:

There are two things that are too amazing for me,
two that I do not understand:
the way of spiritual youths
who become sceptical in adult life;
the way of rebellious youths
who become religious in adult life.

The Dark Side of Reflection

Reflection
Not light, bouncing off
A glossy surface
But a bending back
A reaching deep within
Pulling out bygone memories
Memories of people, events
Happenings of long ago
Forget forgetfulness
Even when you have
Chosen to forget
Bring them all back
Bend over backwards
And see again

Toying with memory
Turning it over
Chewing it gently
Ruminating, brooding
Lost connections, looking
Startling disclosures, revealing

Neural pathways, creating
Reordering events
Reassessing persons
Re-imagining reality
But what if
All this reflecting
Conjures up fantasy
Inventing fantastic non-happenings?

Glory Awaits

Bloodied hands
Hold firmer
Swollen eyes
Never cease to see

Battered body
Continues the climb
For at the mountaintop
Awaits glory

The Future Looks Fantastic

The future looks bleak
No, wait, change the filter
There you go
The future looks fantastic
Zoom in, damn pixelation
Perhaps, then
Blurry is future's name?

Wait a minute
What picture are you photoshopping?
Have you really a snapshot of tomorrow?
How on earth can you click
Let alone capture, the future?

Is it not all a lie? A big fat invention?
False soothsaying, empty predictions!
Researched projections and prognostications
Big data analysis and tabulations!
Just look at the weather forecasts!

Can we ever talk of the future
Without being chained to the now?

Perhaps the chains are longer
Disappearing into the deep bygones
To which they are moored and held fast?

Wait, if we can't access the future
Can the future not call out?
Can it not reach out to fill our minds
With wonders, fantasies, marvels
And many unthought dreams?

Can we not imagine?
Surely, we can creatively divine
Perhaps even respond, reaching out
To the unseeing invisible beyond
And grab the uncaptured
And as we clutch at it
May we not boldly paint our faces on it?

The Worlds of Texts

Tossed back and forth
By the raging sea of pages
Swept upon different shores
Strange sites, exotic places

Living in the land of Aslan and the White Witch
Riding alongside Turgut, Bamsi, Ertugrul
Swinging swords with Hector and Achilles
Cave-hopping with the Sons of Zeruiah and David

In the battlefield with Karna, Arjuna, Krishna
Following the great Alexander of Macedonia
To the ends of the world with the Hobbits
Or just simply walking upon the waters

Never straying too far
Never to stay too long
Dragged back by the ebbing waves
Its mesmerizing, beckoning tales
Alas! Only to be tossed back
And forth, all over again

Preserving Our Ancestors

Restrictions of one's tradition,
artistic, religious or cultural,
make possible the preservation
of one's ancestral inheritance

In following one's art tradition,
one is restricted by the ancestor's
styles, forms and techniques

Only by preserving these restrictions
one is able to provide sanctuary
to one's ancestral theory of beauty

And yet, the artist has the freedom
to interpret and innovate,
to make her ancestors
relevant to present days

Pathways Without Purpose

I have been robbed
Brutally betrayed
Morning after morning, forced
With religious fervour and fire
On pathways without purpose
On drives without destinations
On roads without targets

Oh, give back my childhood
The strength of my youth
I will carve out my own path
With the sickle and the flute
But do tell me where to go
Destinations, purpose and targets
Give me the order, I will get there

What paths and roads
Or highways to take
Northward or south
Perhaps, westwards, east
Leave it to the sun
Glistening on the morning dew
The roads will beckon my feet

Morning Drive

Rising with emptiness
Racing eyes, longing soul
Drag me through
Dangerous dark alleyways
And along sweet
Country roads
Straining, searching
Yet never ever finding

Descending Jacob's Ladder

Youth fades into frailty
Like a spent rocket cracker
Which once lit
Swiftly climbs up Jacob's ladder

With the strength of a thousand horses
Loud as a marauding army
Lighting up the night sky
Driving darkness away

Reaching a crescendo
Erupts a splash of colours
From horizon to horizon
Youth reigneth over all

But soon after the burst
Strength ebbs and lights dim
Spent, returns to a land unknown
The darkness drives back with glee

From Dawn to Dusk

Rise up with the Dawn
Riding the Rays of the Rising Sun
Overtaking the *Riders of the Night*

But for now
Allow the Dusk to bask you
Let the Darkness envelop you

In the Belly of the Earth
In the deep dark furnace
With Patience, with Perseverance

Learn to Ride the Sunrays
To Dance in the Moonlight
And to Drive the Darkness away

Living with Endings

Endings are sad!
End of an era is sadder!
Change of the old guard
Can be torturous!

Leaving and moving on is sad!
Death is saddest!
And yet, life goes on
Or so it is said!

I don't think life just goes on!
A part of life ends with
every ending, leaving and dying
We lose pieces of ourselves
with every going away, ending

Life does go on,
but in a rather diminished manner
That is why, endings
Leavings and deaths matter
We need to respect endings
Give them their due grieving!

So that after the grieving
We can begin to walk again
Even if it is only
Learning to plod on

Questing Questioning Faith

Anyone serious about religion and faith
Needs to be deeply interested
In questions that probe
The conditions of faith!
Being superstitiously religious
On a Sunday only reveals a lack of faith!

Therefore, here are some questions:
What is truth?
Whom do we believe?
How can we be certain of truth?
The underlying question
Behind these questions:
On what basis do we accept
Something as undisputed true knowledge,
So that everything contrary
Can be termed as false?
Also, furthermore
Is true knowledge universally valid
Or relative to particular contexts?
A bunch of questions to keep faith alive!
Go on, let's have a little think!

Meaning-making Animals

Humans are meaning-making animals
when they stop making meaning
people doze off!
This is for speakers, preachers,
writers and anyone who
wishes to share wisdom
the moment you stop making sense,
the audience leaves for wonderland!
Interestingly, inversely,
those who do not even have much to say,
When they say it meaningfully
They get a full house!
Think of all our stand-up comedians,
Social media bloggers
YouTubers and Instagrammers
They say little
But filled with meaning
They have all of us hooked!

Amazing Humans (Us)

We take great efforts
To hide our vulnerabilities,
Failures and shortcomings
While all the time
Showcasing our pretence,
Made-up or actual 'good side'!
We are constantly looking
For appreciation,
Validation and acceptance,
hence in everything we put out
we seek to generate
the 'awe' and the 'aww',
the feel-good 'like'
and the happy emojis
from both friends and followers.
Perhaps what we actually
need and require is
may be something quite different.

Bright Sun, Darkened Clouds

Enjoy the bright sun and blue skies
But be grateful for the clouds
Both in poetry and literature
the imagery of a
Bright sun and blue skies
are used to convey
the idea of life's goodness,
hope and vibrancy
While clouds often darkened
represent gloom, despair and doom

Lord Byron's 'The Dream'
A perfect example:
And they were canopied by the blue sky,
So cloudless, clear, and purely beautiful

Even as I look out of the window,
On this cloudless morning,
I too see blue skies and the glorious sun;
surely it does something within
to lift one's spirit.
It energizes us

to get up and act
as well as to be sat
basking in its beauty

But I have not forgotten
the darkened clouds
and the blinding storms,
of the not-too-distant past
I dare not forget them,
they too taught many lessons.
Even if difficult,
I have learnt to be grateful for them.
Bright shining sun,
blue skies as well as dark clouds
with blinding rains
all knit together
the fabric of our lives
this brief passage through time.

The Godfather: A Tribute

The Godfather tells a rich story. Few stories in our history have been better told.

A story of
rags to riches,
crime to high office,
nexus between
religion and the underworld,
and about
the messiness of raising a family
even as it spills
over to the next generations,
with all the drama that
only an Italian family can bring—
family above business,
but loyalty above family.
Love and murder,
even of one's own brother,
treachery of close friends,
forbidden loves,
and offers that cannot be refused.
If Mario Puzo wrote well,
then Francis Ford Coppola directed better.

Marlon Brando, Al Pacino,
Diane Keaton, Robert De Niro,
Andy Garcia, Sofia Coppola,
just to name a few,
set the screen on fire
And yet, it is the story of one man,
the journey of one man—
scion of the greatest crime family,
who gives it all up
to go to war on behalf of his country and
returns a decorated war hero.
But gets dragged centre stage
of the crime world
with the assassination attempt
on his father's life.
From then on,
it is a story
about the paradox
of this man's life
who seeks catharsis,
with his eyes set on
getting out of crime
and yet the plot takes him
only deeper in, and
further into the dark murky waters
of the underworld,

pulled strongly by Puzo and Coppola!
But how do we end such a story!
Plots get rewritten,
in search of the perfect
pathos-filled finale.
Death is too easy a way out
for Michael Corleone—
the father of all Godfathers.
Death wouldn't bring enough pain,
so Coppola and Puzo
kill his beloved daughter,
the apple of his eye!
Perhaps, in that tragic scene
we have reached
the full height of pathos
a tragedy is meant to bring,
as imagined by Aristotle himself.
Dust to dust,
death to death,
nothing to nothing.
The world ends.
Michael too finally dies
in Corleone,
leaving behind an empty echo
of nothingness.
His catharsis never came.

He probably
never truly repented.
It leaves a void,
an emptiness,
and the viewer suffers in silence.
The plot has taken over,
and the true mourning
is in the knowledge
that the story
that must go on,
will never take off again.
The story has been abandoned.
The catharsis that must come
will never come.
Thus, the faithful viewer concludes—
perhaps,
in a re-watching,
just one more time,
we might wrestle Michael over
and receive the catharsis
that he so desperately sought.
Perhaps, this time around,
we may attain it.
And the reruns continue.

The Line Between Good and Evil

It is said
that there is a thin line
between good and evil.
This is especially true
of the flags we fly
and the causes we champion.
Our allegiance and support,
to entities and causes,
while noble and good,
if they go beyond a certain point
or get narrowly focused
then these same well-intentioned
support schemes and allegiances
can turn to the dark side

For example,
while support for child rights is good,
overly enthusiastic support
for child rights
can turn negative
towards parental care

and family structure.
Similarly, patriotism to one's country
or people group is good,
however,
a narrow and exclusive patriotism
can lead to political fundamentalism
and tribalism
which are hugely detrimental

One way to avoid these mishaps
can be to locate our cause
in the larger matrix
of causes and human life,
and then give it
its honest due
weighing in our support

There is no need
to pit one cause
against another
Rather understand
Our favourite cause
In light of all others
Support many, even diversity
Even as you love one
The one you support

Uncomfortable Conversations

I heard the phrase
Uncomfortable conversations
in a conversation this evening
It made me pause
and wonder!
I had never really
thought about or reflected deeply
on this theme before!

Immediately a few questions
came up in my mind:
What are uncomfortable conversations?
In contrast, what are comfortable conversations?
Why do conversations become uncomfortable?
What are the characteristics
of uncomfortable conversations?
What are the benefits,
if any, of uncomfortable conversations?
What is the goal here?
Is it to transform
uncomfortable conversations

into comfortable conversations?
Or do uncomfortable conversations
Transform us
And in the discomfort
Bring comfort?

Wise Living

I wish there was!
But there is none
No 'one size fits all'
grand and perfect model
for our human life.
Just like no two
fingerprints are alike,
similarly,
no two life paths are similar.
But is that not the beauty of life?
To be able to discover,
imagine, create and find
our path in the world—
is that not precisely
what it means to be human?
This does not mean
'anything goes!'
There are traditions
handed down to us
about every aspect of life.
And yet,

being human
is to take the best
and to innovate the rest!
Cheers to wise living!

Power of Words

Words are powerful.
Once uttered,
like an arrow
that has left the bow,
they cannot be recalled
or taken back.
They possess
tremendous power
to do evil
or bring about justice.
Perhaps that is why
it is said,
'be quick to listen
and slow to speak'
Being careful with our words
is good for both ourselves
as well as everyone else.
Practically, I learnt this a long time ago,
whenever there is the urge
or impulse to speak or react,
it is precisely at those moments
that we need to keep silent.
Allow the moment,

of frenzy and
of heightened emotions,
to pass over
and then reflect
on the situation at hand
with a clear head.
It is only after that
we should articulate
a worthy response,
a wise choosing of words
carefully
so that our words
will not only represent us well,
but also bring healing
and justice
to those who hear.

At Death

At death,
our earth-framed existence
completely ends,
and hence,
all we have is this life
after which there is nothing

At death,
the body dies
but the soul
continues to exist

At death,
the soul immediately
becomes a part
of a universal consciousness
and loses its individuality.

At death,
the soul migrates
from one life-form
to another
and the migrations
go on forever.

At death,
the soul migrates
from one life-form
to another
until it breaks
out of the cycle
of life-forms
and becomes a part
of the Universal Consciousness.

At death,
the soul has
a single destiny
(Heaven or its equivalent)
where its individuality
is preserved
for eternity
in a happy place.

At death,
the soul has
a destiny (Heaven or Hell)
that is contingent
on the kind of life
it lived on earth.

Be Empowered

Empower your neighbour!
Receiving power
from the care of others
is a gift, an honour,
and a huge privilege.
Let us receive with gratitude!

The care can be
in the form of
food and water,
a word of encouragement,
wisdom or even rebuke,
and love
in its multitudinous forms.

The opportunity to
empower our neighbour
by giving them our care
is a great calling,
an honour and a huge privilege.
Let us care with love.

Is not power and energy,
life itself?
Empowering then is
nothing less than life-giving!
We have the incredible
opportunity and power
to both give
and receive life
from one other.
Be Empowered!

Time Is Slipping, Did You Know

Time is slipping
Did you know
Time is slipping away fast
The characters we play
The stories we partake
And the desires we crave
Are they worthy of our time?
Time is slipping
Did you know
Time is slipping away fast
People with whom we tango
Should we rather let go
To be with those
With whom we will further go
Time is slipping
Did you know
Time is slipping away fast
Have you dreamt
To be part of an unending world
A young world that never grows old
No warts and all

No till death do us apart
And yet, time is slipping
Did you know
Time is slipping away fast

Worthy Lives

Thoughts and desires no one sees

Words people hear
Actions people may see

A worthy life

Not one that adheres
To rulebooks or religious norms
But one that is consistent in its
Thoughts, desires, words and deeds

A murderous thief
Consistent with
Thieving imaginations
And thievery acts
A corrupt politician
Consistent with
Selfish ambition
And self-centred behaviour
A lying businessman
Consistent with
Boastful pride
And clever manipulations

Continue to live
Worthy lives

Destinations of Meaning

If life cannot be measured merely by time
Then is life also about the distance covered?
If life can also be measured by distance
Then how does one value the covered distance?

If distance by time gives speed
Then perhaps life is better measured
By speed rather than mere time or distance
If speed is more distance in less time
Then how do we measure
The value of one's speed of life?
Perhaps it is the directions one takes
As well as the destinations at which one arrives
Could they determine the value of life?

What good is distance
Without direction?
What good is direction
Without destination?
What good is distance, time and speed
Without directions and destinations?

If by directions
We mean decisions
And by destinations
We mean meaningful spaces
Then the speed of life
That determines
The quality of life
Must be reimagined

If speed is not just
Covering distance by time
And valuable life speed lies in
Distance covered towards
Meaningful spaces
Then a valuable life is nothing but
The distance covered
In decisioned directions
To destinations of meaning

On Truth, Interpretation and Lies

TRUTH reveals reality
Nothing right or wrong about it!
It is a revelation
One directly experiences
Truth is not spoken
Only manifested

INTERPRETATIONS are messages
About reality
They involve the subjectivity
Of the messenger
As well as
The objective reality
They seek to represent

Therefore, everything
That is said or spoken
By a human
Is an interpretation
If all speech is interpretation
The goal of interpretations
Then is twofold—

To communicate
As faithfully as possible
The objective reality
One has received or experienced
While equally acknowledging
That what one says
Is always limited
By one's subjective understanding
Language and experience

We therefore have
Better interpretations
And bad interpretations
Depending on the accuracy
Of our communication
And representation
Of the objective reality
One has experienced

LIES are simply
Wrong interpretations.
Lies are conscious speech
That seek to conceal
The manifested truth
As well as
Negate one's experience.
Lies have intentional motives
To deceive and misrepresent

Bottom line
Truth is manifested
And revealed
We experience it
When we speak about it
We interpret
When we seek to
Interpret wrongly
To hide and conceal
Then we lie

Phoenix Rising from the Ashes

Look at the happy messes
We make in life
This is the reality
Of our lives
While we all hate
Mistakes and accidents
They are very much part
Of our human condition

A constant obsession
With being perfect
Makes human existence
Unenjoyable and torturous

However, messes,
However silly
Are still messes
And they bring hurt, pain
Bitterness and sadness

Although we can genuinely
Apologize and seek forgiveness

The pain or the brokenness
May never leave

Therefore, while we learn
To live with this broken
Human condition
Can we not do something
Proactively to minimize
This sad side of our existence?

What comes out of us
At that impulsive moment,
Be it an action, a word, or a thought
Comes out of us
Because they have found a home
Within us already

Therefore, constantly reflecting
On what kind of thoughts
Habits and practices
Have found a home
Within us
And a constant detoxification
Of our inner self
As well as actively
Instilling within us
Healthy thoughts
Words and habits

Are perhaps ways to ensure
That we are developing
An acceptable character
Which then will bring forth
Hopefully and surely
Good, acceptable and wise
Words, thoughts and actions
At that impulsive unguarded moment

And yet, however
We seek to rectify
Our broken condition
Remember the world
Too is broken
Other humans are also broken
And a lot of brokenness
Is not in our control

Therefore, as part of
Being human
We all will regularly
Face brokenness and sadness
Perhaps, the real lesson here
Is in learning
To pick ourselves up and walk
And even run, again

This Is It

Don't listen to the fantasies
that your mind spins,
but listen to your body!
Your body that occupies
a certain space
in a certain time
knows very well
that life is just
this fleeting existence—
the unrepeatable act of living,
directed towards death.

The mind is deluded
and assumes that
we will live forever.
As the mind can
replay memories,
it gives the illusion
that life will repeat itself,
and that we can
always go back
to a previous state.
The mind makes us forget

that life is unrepeatable,
and that once lived,
we are never to relive
that moment
which was lived.

Therefore, THIS IS IT!
Today will never
come back again.
This moment we share
will soon forever be gone!
The opportunity that today presents
will never come back.
The people you meet now,
you will never meet again.

Hence, we must have the attitude
of 'This is it'
which will enable us
to make the most of the 'Now'.
Having the attitude of 'This is it'
will also set us free
to relish and enjoy every moment,
without being distracted
either by memories of the past
or by imaginations of the future.
THIS IS IT!

Surviving Youth

Childhood was innocence
Perhaps not all of it
But as we stepped
Into youthfulness
Our young hearts
Began to melt
Bodies changed
Feelings sprung
Took form
Of the forms they met

Suffered great pangs
Of sorrow and love
A thousand deaths
They have endured
Writhing in pain
Twisting with agony
Shattered and broken
A million pieces on the
Crystal glass floor

It's been a long time
Since youth passed
But all I have been

Doing ever since is
Trying to put back together
The pieces strewn in shreds
Recovering and rehabilitating
Surviving the dark terrors
Set in motion ages ago
O the flesh-peeling
Claws of youth

O Ancient of Days

I am a traveller, an adventurer,
A discoverer of new worlds!
I will make my bed
On the mountaintops
And my habitat
On the deep sea rocks
The lion will be my friend
The falcon my eyes
The trees my companions
And the green grass my allies
The fiery sun will guide me by day
And the red moon by night
The wind that fills my lungs
Will burst forth with eternal sounds
I am the seer and the seen
The runner who is run upon
The trampler of the beast
Riding it by its wild horns
I have seen the morning star fall
And heard its mighty trembling
Your ordained narrative

Ceaselessly unfolding
Endlessly declarative
Matchlessly interpretative
O Ancient of Days!

Under the Sun's Warm Gaze

Don't chase what
Doesn't fall straight
The wind, your ally
Sifting the chaff away
While gravity, the foe
Drawing unlovables close

What is meant to be
will always fall near
finding its way
by your side
What isn't meant to be
Even if by your side
Will soon get blown away
To lands far, far away

Now, planted by your side
Gravity, too, pulling deeper
Winds bringing food and water
Friend and foe working together
All under the sun's warm gaze
Growing stronger and brighter

Under the canopy offering shade
And shelter, a home to rest
In the evening of life
Humming the swan's majestic song

Enough Is Enough

He stormed into the house
Dropped himself on the floor
And there he lay
What seemed like forever
Motionless, without sound,
Almost breathless

Jumped to his feet
Leapt off the ground
In a blind fury
That rocked the house
Grabbed a pen
Wrote furiously on the wall

'Enough Is Enough!'
The words read
Etched in blood
Beaming out of the wall

Flinging the pen
Splattering ink everywhere
Stomping up and down
A wild elephant become, had he
Nataraja on a spree
With Shambhu taking over

The moment of reckoning
Had finally arrived
Why such hostility
Why such fervour
'Every Slim Shady
Please stand up
Please stand up'
Do give an account
Before we let bygones be bygones

He slumped back on the floor
Haggard and motionless
The faraway look was back
Without sound, almost breathless
With head hung low
Limping and dragging
Standing back on his feet

Yelling at the Lil' Fella

Yelling at
The lil' fella
Is the easiest
Thing to do
One can thunder
Raise hell and
High water
No resistance
Not even defiance

Easily beaten
Into subjection
The lil' fella'
Cringes in fear
Shuddering, he
Cowers and recoils
Trembling, shrinking
Wishing to be invisible

His body takes the pain
As well as the shame
Never saying no to blame
Always willing to be framed

Even to be maimed
All excuses found lame
Destined to be tame

Masters to servants
Mistresses to maids
Teachers to students
Managers to aides
Guests to waiters
Foremen to workers
Even parents to children

What joy in shaming
What pleasure in maiming
What grandeur in framing
What grandness in taming
What praise in subjugating
What glory in yelling

You want glory
Empower the lil' fella
You want praise
Lift him on high
In his rising
You are raised
In his glory
You get crowned

So, stop
Yelling
At the
Lil' fella

The Seer and the Seen

Reduced
Instrumentalized
A tool for sight
Have you made me

But I am
Nay, eye am
Both the seer
And the seen
Both the receiver
And the revealer
Perceiving all appearance
I uncover my world

Eye am
A window into
An invisible world
A tunnel head
Into a world of nothings

Yet from within
My darkness, emerges
Figures, features and frames
The invisible made visible

The unmanifest, manifest
Nothing becomes something
Mind, thought and soul
The world of invisibles
Becomes flesh
In me, within me, through me

The Hour of the Moon

Inspired by hearing the story of an 87-year-old grandfather who, despite losing his pension, demonstrates self-reliance by collecting and selling agri-products. While his children and grandchildren try to make him stop, he is not willing to take their charity and is eager to be independent. I am sure all of us have people in our lives whose qualities we can celebrate. The world has many unsung heroes, like this dear grandfather, who through their resolve continue to inspire all of us.

Frail is the body
But the spirit strong
The sun of life has set
With all its glories at rest
Capacities have ceased
And strengths have ebbed

Yet the spirit
In resilience abides
Untethered, unfettered
With full freedom and rights
Seeks out resources
Self-sustenance, the aim

Self-preservation, survival,
Self-protection, the game

It's the hour
Of the moon
The age beyond
The setting sun
It's a life that is lived
Between dusk and dawn

Like the sun that blazes
Across the sky
Lighting up
Every dark night

Same does the moon
Striding bright and strong
Unhinged from the sun
Moons up the night sky

Bigger Than

The universe is bigger than all of us
It is bigger than the farthest galaxy
It is bigger than all of life put together
And yes, it is bigger than
The biggest of human egos!
Similarly, the university is bigger than all of us
It is bigger than all the students put together
It is bigger than everything else that gets added in
And yes, it is bigger than everyone's ego!
Surplus, extra, excess
Those are the words used
To describe the fullness and bigness
Of the whole, always more,
Than the sum of its parts
Of both the universe and the university
He who has ears
Let him hear
He who has eyes
Will definitely see

Sunrays

My Original!

With the sunrays
Caressing my face
And the cool breeze
Fumbling along
The grey mountains
Line up my horizon
And the deep blue sky
Spreads out my tent
O what a beautiful world
I am yours and you mine

ChatGPT's Improvisation!

As sun rays gently grace my face,
And cool breeze softly dances in place,
The mighty mountains, grey and strong,
Line up my horizon all day long.
The deep blue sky above spreads wide,
A canvas of beauty, never to hide,
And as I lay in my humble tent,
I am awed by the world, so magnificent.
O what a wondrous place to be,

In awe of nature, so wild and free,
I am yours, and you are mine,
Forever bound, in love divine.

Move the World

It's a short ride, and
Everyone drives with pride
But no one drives forever
Even if there will always be
Profound untamed pleasure

But in this moment
I have choices to make
Roads to choose
Paths to take

The less travelled
Or the most entertained

Who will I meet
I do not know
What will I do
I never would know
Desires, reasons,
Expectations, obligations
All want to drive
Let's say—take me for a ride

But in every step I take
In every word I say

In every moment I be
A new revelation
A manifestation
A powerful expression
I am
Without a lever and a fulcrum
I shall move the world

Chains or Chase

Till dawn, before the sun breaks free
From her shackles of the night
The hunter swiftly after her prey
Over hills and across mountain heights

Wading across wild waters grey
Her eye solely on her prey
The hunter neither waits nor delays
Pursues hotly on the chase

From dawn until rising dusk
The sun now shackled to the day
In spite of the radiant blazing light
The chase continues without respite

Chains for one, chase for the other
The story unfolds from day to day
While some remain shackled all life
Others eternally pursue the chase

A Kite, Boat and Us

Shackled and moored
We always are
Like a kite
To its thread
A train
To its rails
Like a tree in the breeze
A fish in a bottle
Little movements allowed
Within limits may wander

The only difference
From and between
A kite, boat and us
For the unprisoned
Mortals, gay and free
Is in the power
To unshackle and re-shackle
Oneself and the other

To move between shackles
Some chosen, some given
To surrender, to give in
And yet, always trying

To find, looking fervently
For spaces and places
To be utterly free
In between shackles

So Be It!

I embrace all of God's creation
The good, the bad and the ugly
The human and the non-human
The animate and the inanimate
The primitive and the technological
The rocks, the rivers and the flow of information.

If this embrace
Makes the human
Subservient to creation,
Then so be it!

If this embrace
Dethrones the human
And relegates her to
An inconsequential servant
In the project of attaining God,
Then so be it!

In the process of reaching God
If the human species
Is required to undergo kenosis
And be destined to oblivion,
Then so be it!

If God is to be
Truly all in all
And the annihilation
Of the Homo sapiens
Be the necessary sacrifice,
Then so be it!

If it is only when
Humanity lays itself
On the sacrificial altar
So that the next stage
of reaching God
Is achieved,
Then so be it!

I Believe

The sun is a red ball of fire
Going down the hill
Retiring for the night
The breeze that was blowing strong
Suddenly stops
Standing still
Watching the sun go down

The sun has now set
And darkness envelops a'grand
The breeze has become a wind
Blowing a storm across the land

But I believe
It won't be long
Before the sun rises again
And the breeze will become a wind
Blowing the darkness away

The sea is all-powerful
Encompasses within it mountains
Dark and beautiful
Who has seen its depths?
And who has measured its breadth

Every day as dawn turns to dusk
The waves reach higher and higher
Reaching for the sky
Lashing out in fury
Drag down the sun
Swallow it and all light is dead

Through the night
The sea reigns supreme
Throwing tantrums
Dancing waves doing their victory march

But I believe, oh yes, I believe
No dark wave, no fierce night
Can forever keep out my light
My sun will soon shine forth again

Forgiveness

As I gaze at myself
I see the scars of old
Wounds by people inflicted
Opening up and unfold

But when I lift up my eyes to you
On your blood-clad face, I gaze
All my pain fades
In the cruel radiance of your face
Pains I have cherished
Deep down within my heart
Hurts I have nurtured
That have brought me to this lot

As I look at your thorn-crowned head
And gaze at your slap-cheeked face
Your penetrating voice stirs deep within
'Father forgive them' resounds
Demanding my response
Falling to my knees
I say, I plead
Forgive me too as I forgive

Friendship

I opened the door
And walked out
To hear the music
Of my soul
I couldn't hear no strings
Nor any drumbeats
No pipe organ to fill my heart
Nor any trumpet blasts

But as I listened carefully
I could hear
A faint playing of a flute
Full of sorrow and worry
Flowing from the corner of my soul
No happy thoughts
No cheerful feelings
A heavy heart
Laden with burden

In this desperate moment
I thought of friendship
The beauty of two becoming one
The bass and soprano

Blending in a song
Complementing, supplementing
Encouraging, adjusting
Caressing, loving

The commitment to sing together
Is what friendship is all about
Singing, with a cold
Or even with a broken voice

Thank you, friend, for choosing
To sing life with me
Let our song grow richer
As the days go by
And our voices stronger
As the years go by
Let the music of our lives
Reach out to touch
A hurting heart
And bring joy
In the midst of pain

Christmas

The angels were thrilled
When they saw the babe
The shepherds came running
To offer their praise
The wise men adored
With the gifts they gave
On bended knee
The star too was beaming
Peeping into the cowshed

But where is the Father?
Where is the one
Whose son had been born

While the whole universe was rejoicing
Deep sadness filled the Father's heart
As his gaze shifted from the
Cradle to the cross

Uncontrollable joy
Burst on his face
Seeing you and me
At the foot of the cross

Interstitial Spaces

I recall a time
Long time ago
Not quite like 1948
But definitely 1984
Every animal had a role
Every human his place

Classes and companies
Drafted we were
Either by birth
Or chosen roles

We laboured through the day
And even through the night
Siloed and confined
Within our chosen plights

Then arose the morning star
Liberalization, globalization
With life's growing complexities
Tech breakthroughs every day

But the planet was beginning to suffer!

Not just building bridges
Or railroads in far-off lands
Safe water at home, healthy bodies too
And social connections, side by side

Platforms for work and shopping
Knowing desires and needs
Technology shaping our wants
Fulfilling all of our creeds

Technology must know people
Their tastes and their ways
It must know all the spaces
Both public and private places.

Now we must extend our reach
Beyond our own trained domains
To walk and grasp new knowledge
Weaving the new and old in our minds

Only with the help I receive
From others' wisdom and grace
Can I successfully accomplish
What was never wholly mine

As an engineer or a technologist
I can surely achieve new heights
Grasp what is needed to build
Only when your path entwines with mine

The Poet

A poet must begin
Where he is
In the earthy mansion
Shrouding his life

In order to understand
Where people are
Their lived experiences
Moulded with time
Clayed in space

And then take them
On the wings
Of his words
Clinging
To the heartbeat
Of his soul
To a new world
Where he himself
Wants to be

Sojourning Beyond Stories

You liberated me
You gave me life
You freed me from the chains
No mere facts or logic's strife
But you, dear narrative
You defined who I am

The freedom I embraced
On that wondrous day,
Still lingers in my senses,
In each gasp and inner nod,
In the deep widening smiles
The power to steer the plot
To be any character I choose
Twists and turns at my command
The story's mine to use

But stories forge connections
And characters deepen kinships
In the space conquered
Boundary walls erected
Identities take shape

The story stamps its mark
On all that it contains
Restraining, confining
The story takes over
Enslaved to the story
I begin to feel its chains

Oh, where is the freedom
That was promised
The menu of characters
The buffet of plots

The stranglehold tightens
And the noose stiffens
Every move dictated
Every action scripted

All responses curated
Bound by the screenplay
My choices already decided
Structured plots and lines

It is this revelation
This disclosure
About the inner workings
Of stories and narratives
That demanded of me

To break free
From the structures
Of story itself

Unhinged from plots
Breaking away from
All human bonds
I walk away, yet embrace
Untamed realities
Un-storied terrains

Without naming
Without representing
Just being, living
A story-less life

And, this, is my story

Being Engages Knowing

Two ways of knowing
Sensory and reflective
Knowing dictates being
Behold they are born
The scientist and the sage

Science gives knowledge
Of various worlds
Within and without
Theories and laws
Facts and figures
Backed by data

Ordaining and declaring
With Cartesian certitude
Firm knowledge about
This wondrous universe

There is another way
One that gazes inward
Yoga for one
Meditation for another
Closed eyes, silent mouths
Revelation is the goal

In the playground of the mind
In the deep recesses
Of one's consciousness
Mystical intuitive figures dance
Disclosing themselves, revealing knowledge

One with the telescope
Other with her eyes closed
Both declare their claim
To the throne of knowledge

Just as the scientist
With their theories and experiments
Cannot ignore their inner self
So cannot the sage
With their meditations and intuitions
Ignore the outer world

The scientist and the sage
Hence must walk together
Each needs the other
To make meaning
And live wisely
In this complex world

Acknowledgements

I want to express my gratitude to Sreemoyee Bhattacharyya and Arkamita Sengupta for their invaluable editorial support as I began considering the publication of these poems.

Huge appreciation goes to Kelsey Patton for reading the entire manuscript, making the final edits, and for her incisive comments, which have made the manuscript much sharper.

I would like to extend my heartfelt thanks to the entire team at Rupa Publications, especially Dibakar Ghosh, whose belief in my work and unwavering support made this collection's publication possible, and Shatarupa Dhar, whose keen editorial eye, thoughtful guidance and critical inputs helped shape this book into something I am proud to share.

Finally, I am deeply thankful for all the encouragement and support I have received from Plaksha University, which has been instrumental in bringing this book to fruition.